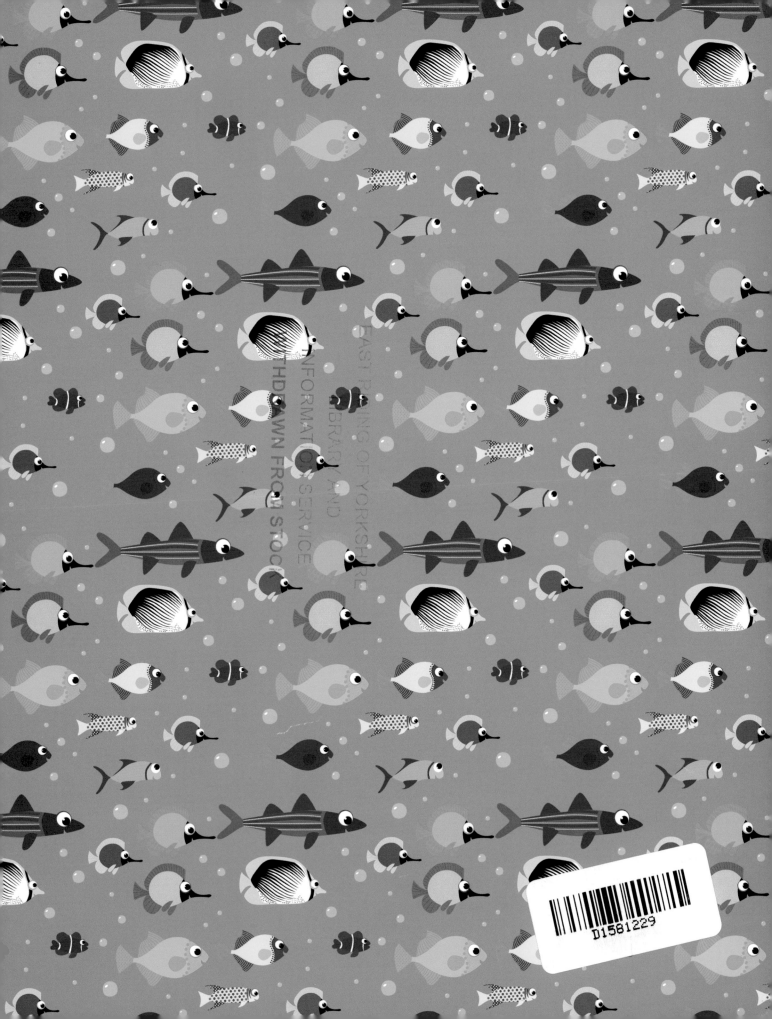

For: Maisey

First published in 2015 by Rockpool Children's Books Ltd.

This edition published in 2015 by Rockpool Children's Books Ltd.
in association with Albury Books.
Albury Court, Albury, Thame
OX9 2LP, United Kingdom

Text and Illustrations copyright © Sam Walshaw 2015

Sam Walshaw has asserted her moral rights
to be identified as the author and illustrator of this work.
© Rockpool Children's Books Ltd. 2015

Printed in China

ISBN 978-1-906081-82-9 (Paperback)

rockpool
children's books

Albury Books

Sam & Maisey Walshaw

Minnie the Minnow &
Jasper
the Jumping Jellyfish

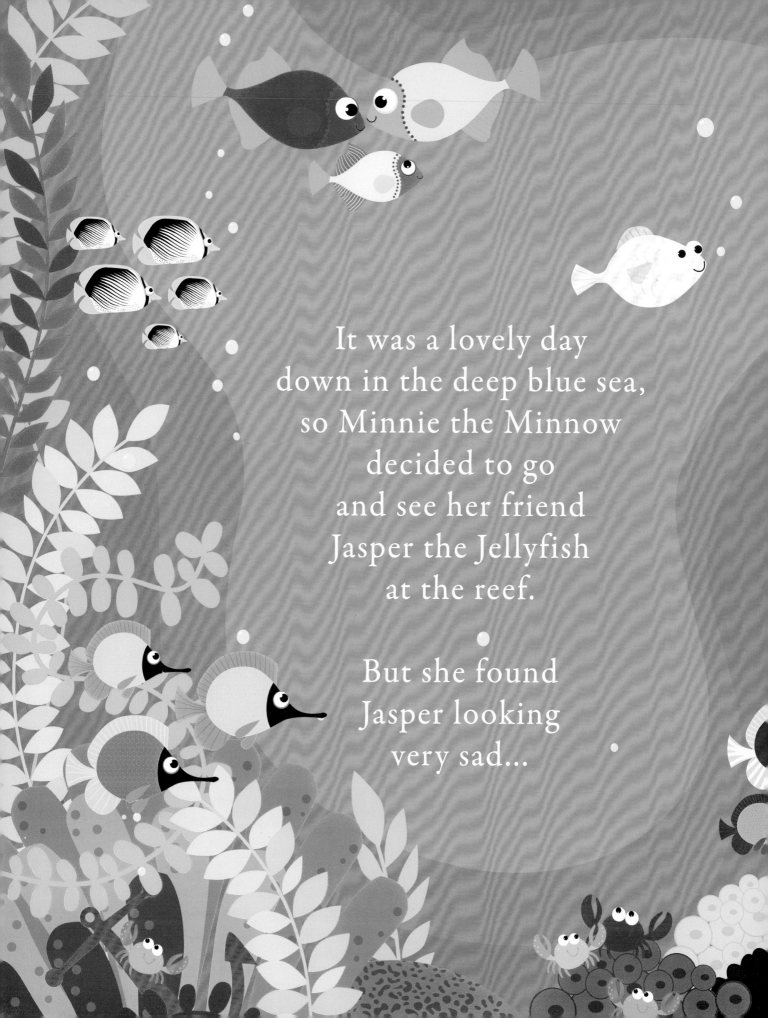

It was a lovely day
down in the deep blue sea,
so Minnie the Minnow
decided to go
and see her friend
Jasper the Jellyfish
at the reef.

But she found
Jasper looking
very sad...

"Whatever is wrong?"
Minnie asked.
"Oh, I feel useless,"
said Jasper.
"I'm just no good at anything.
All I do is swim about all day.
What's the good of that?"

"You are bound to be good at something — everyone is," said Minnie. "We just need to find out what your special thing is!"

"We do?" asked Jasper, brightly.
"Will you help me find
my special thing?"
"I'll be glad to — come on!"
trilled Minnie.

They swam along until
they met Mrs Fish.
"Baby Fish is stuck behind this
rock," she cried. "I'm trying
to get him out, but it's hard
without arms!"

"This is your
chance, Jasper,"
whispered Minnie,
"I bet your tentacles
can get him out."

But when Jasper tried to help,
he got his tentacles caught in the rocks.
"Oh, go away Jasper," snapped Mrs Fish.
"You're useless!"
Jasper swam slowly and sadly
back to Minnie.

A little further on, they met
some fish trying to play football.
"We've got our ball stuck
in the coral," they moaned.
"Go on Jasper," hissed Minnie.
"Help them out."

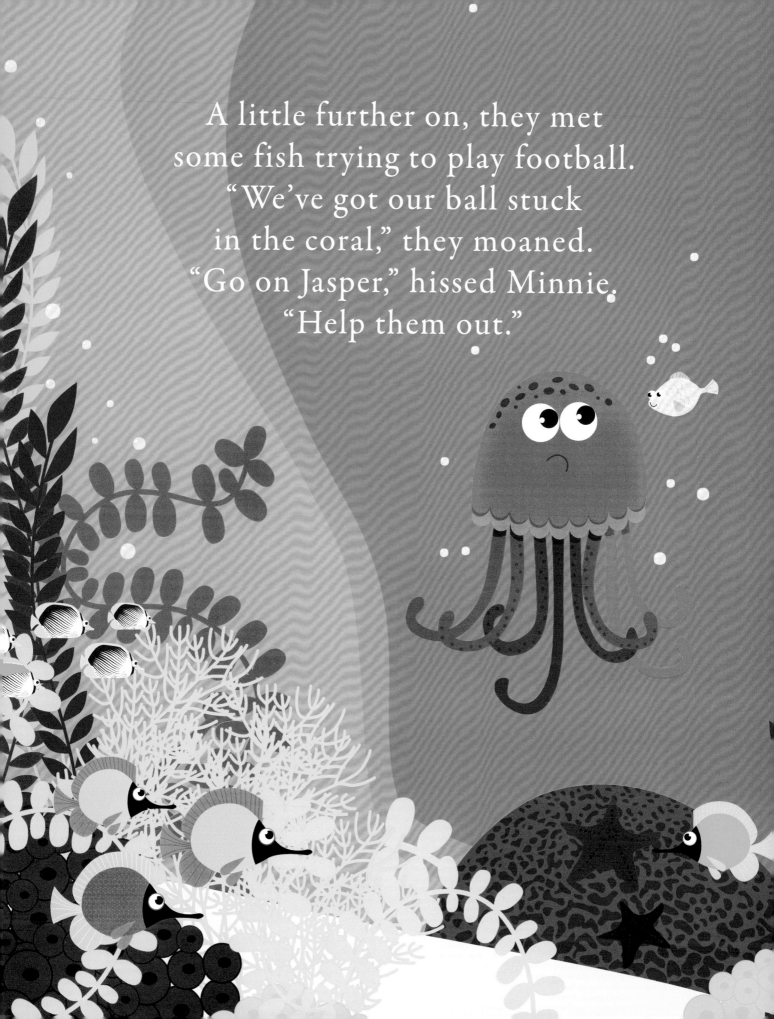

Jasper tried,
but he just poked the ball
further in.
"Oh, go away," chorused the fish.
"You're useless!"
"This isn't going well," thought Minnie.

Jasper looked sadder than ever.
"Don't worry Jasper," Minnie coaxed.
"There must be something you are good at.
We just need to find out what!"

Just past the old treasure chest
they found Turtle with his foot
stuck in some weeds.
"I bet you can help him,"
urged Minnie.
But no: Jasper's tentacles
just tangled the weeds tighter
around Turtle's foot.
"Oh, go away Jasper,"
grunted Turtle,
"You're useless!"

Jasper was downhearted.
"I want to go home now," he said.
"Okay — maybe we can try
again tomorrow," said Minnie.
"Maybe," sighed Jasper.
"But it's no use — just like me."
They began to head home.
But suddenly...

...Minnie and a lot of other fish were scooped up together in a big net. "Minnie!" yelled Jasper.

And then things got even worse — the net began to drag them up to the surface. "Help!" shouted Minnie.

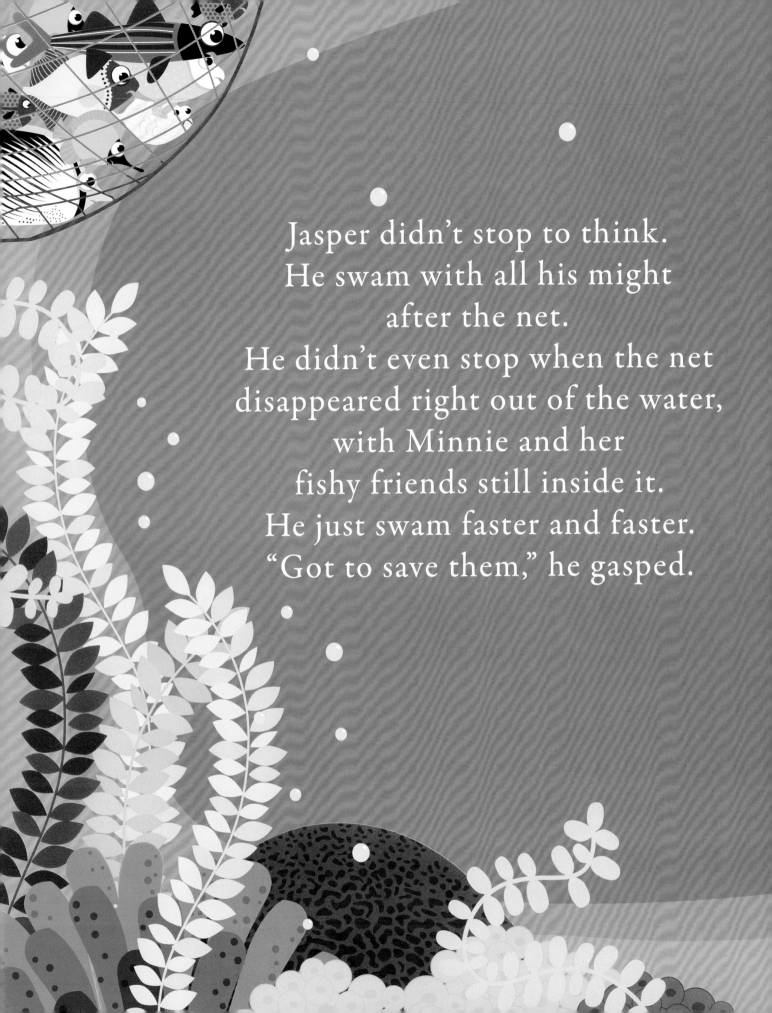

Jasper didn't stop to think.
He swam with all his might
after the net.
He didn't even stop when the net
disappeared right out of the water,
with Minnie and her
fishy friends still inside it.
He just swam faster and faster.
"Got to save them," he gasped.

Suddenly, Jasper was at the surface,
but he just kept going and surged
right out of the water after the net.
Minnie and the other fish were
amazed to see him jump so high.
With his long tentacles
Jasper tore at the net
and let all his friends go.

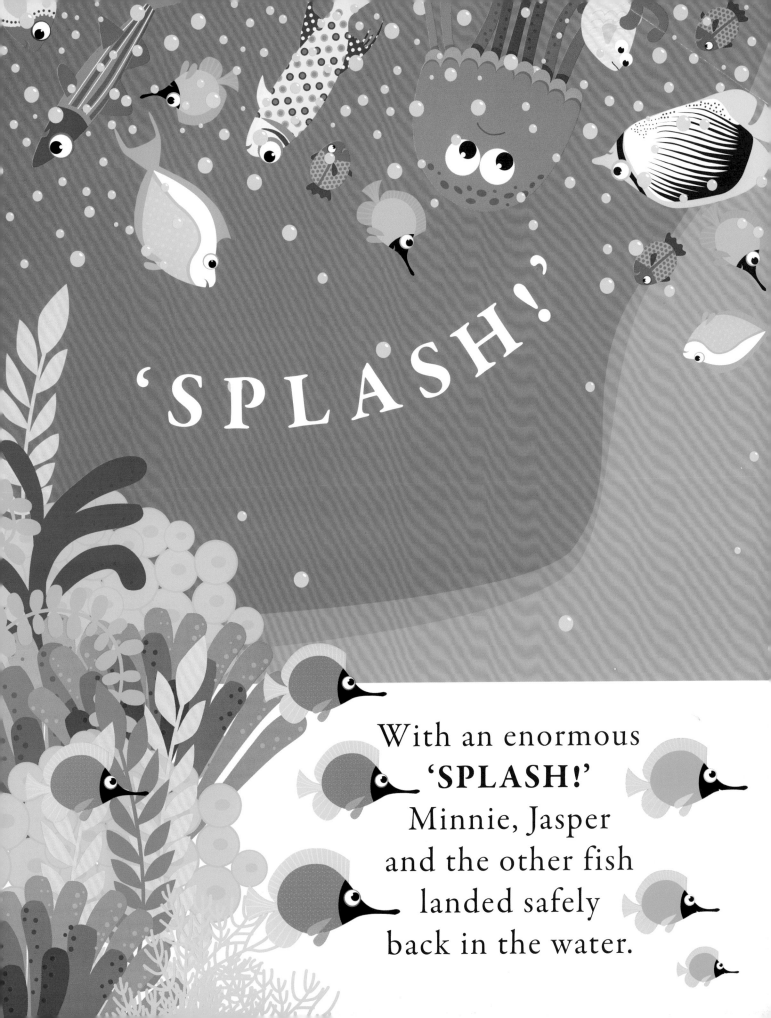

'SPLASH!'

With an enormous **'SPLASH!'** Minnie, Jasper and the other fish landed safely back in the water.

"Wow!" they all chorused.
"We never knew you could jump
like that, Jasper."

"It was amazing,"
gasped Minnie,
"Was it?" said Jasper shyly.

"It WAS!" they laughed.

"So I do have
a special talent,
after all!" he crowed.

Now that everyone knew just what Jasper
could do, he was always in demand.
He helped Baby Crab when
his balloon floated away...

...he jumped out of the water
and brought back
the Turtle Team's football
whenever it went out of play...

...and he gave
the baby fish
jumping rides
in the
school holidays...

...and no one ever told Jasper he was useless
...ever again!

Enjoy another Minnie book in the series!

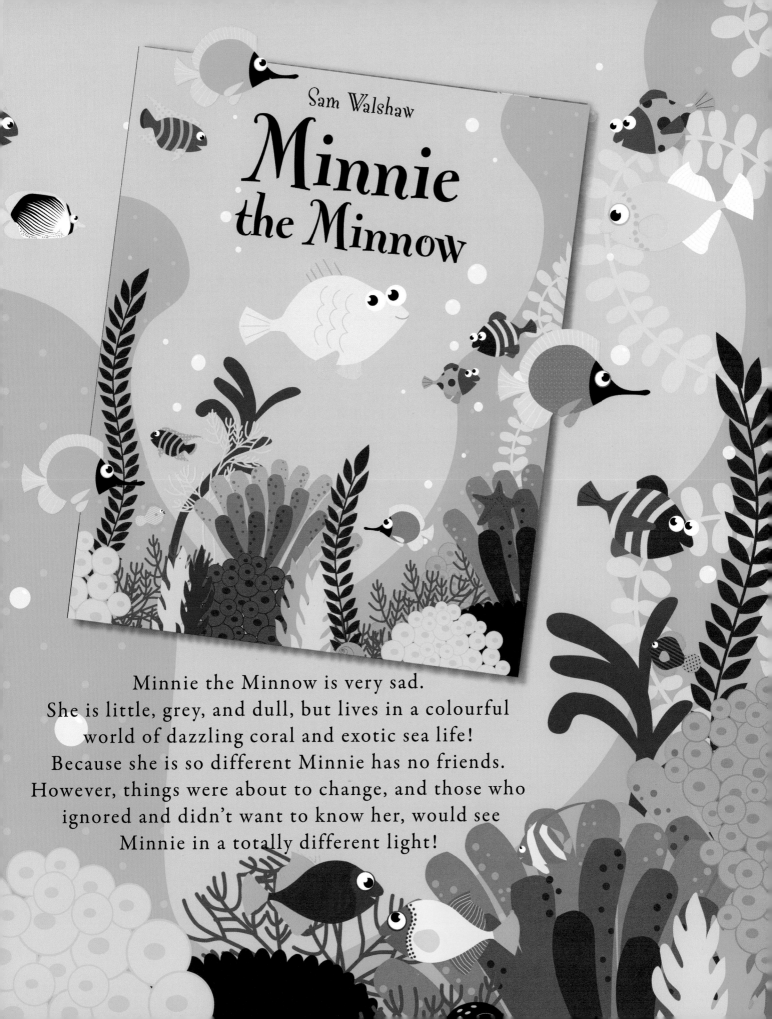

Sam Walshaw

Minnie the Minnow

Minnie the Minnow is very sad.
She is little, grey, and dull, but lives in a colourful
world of dazzling coral and exotic sea life!
Because she is so different Minnie has no friends.
However, things were about to change, and those who
ignored and didn't want to know her, would see
Minnie in a totally different light!

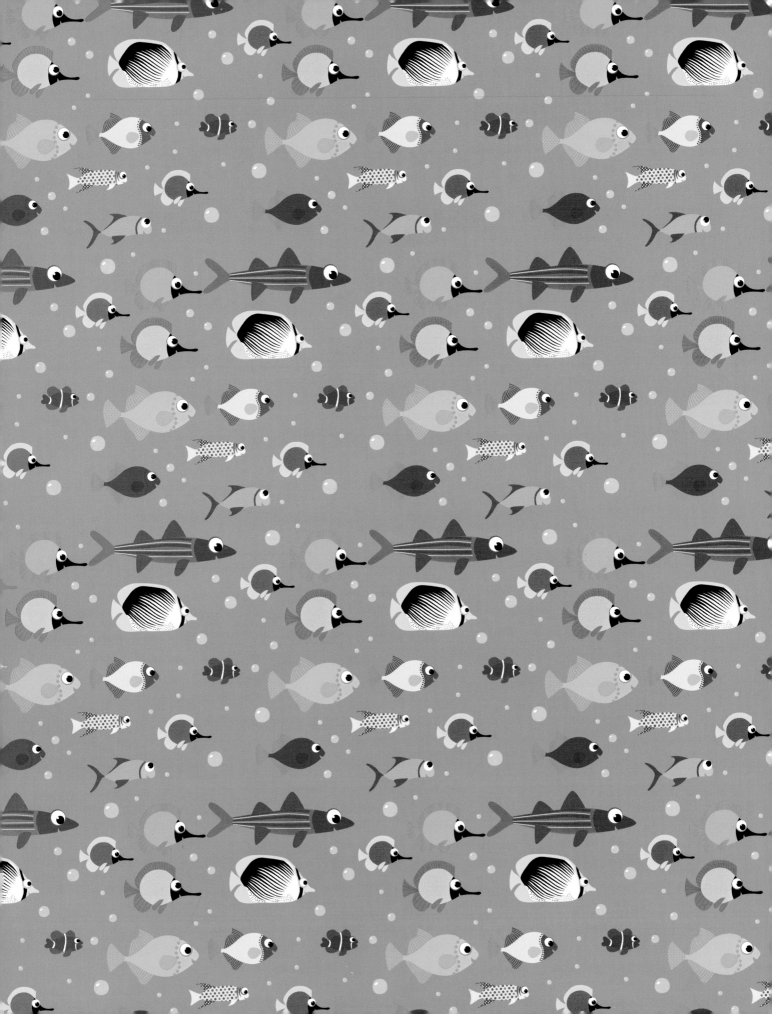